Magic of the Taiga

Sirpa Pursiainen

Copyright © 2016 Sirpa Pursiainen
Publisher: FACE training center
Translation: Sirpa Pursiainen & Christine Puza

ISBN: 978-952-93-8204-0 (nid.)

Foreword

I dedicate this book to all the children and the young-at heart. Life is full of miracles that we see every day, if only we dare.

Beauty in nature is intertwined with day and night, telling us a lot about ourselves and about life in general. Especially in the middle of the rush it is good to stop for a moment to see and hear. Children and fairy tales often provide an important example of the difference between listening and consultation.

Let us have courage to seek and find treasures within us and around us!

As the northern lights appeared in the sky, Grandfather began to tell me a story. They were the first northern lights, which I saw.

Grandfather said: I was born when the northern lights were dancing in the sky. Mother always said that I am wonderfully made. I am as great of a miracle as the northern lights in the firmament.

When I was a cub, I was interested in the world around me. I asked a lot of questions and examined the environment.

Mother and father taught us. In particular, mother taught to look out for danger. Mother warned about angry birds of prey and bears we didn´t know. Mother taught me, and my brother and sister to climb a tree when danger threatens. She also warned us more than once, of an unpredictable evil-pond which makes you hear the things you wish.

When I was little, I often wondered about the things in the world. Our Home Forest seemed so small. Trees that I had never seen interested me immensely. The idea of greater bond than the bond of Home Forest with the big salmon fascinated me tremendously.

Often I dreamily wondered about all the adventures of the world, which my grandfather had told me.

In my mind I had planned my own adventure for a long time. Several times, my mother or father had to bring me home from the edge of the woods, where I directed my steps.

Eventually I convinced my brother to come along for the ride. I promised him that we will find great salmon in the distance. In my mind, I thought that we could keep watch alternately; one awake while the other is asleep.

A day arrived when we left for our adventure. My brother was scared of the dark forest, which opened in the border of the Home Forest. I encouraged him, gave him a hug and said: "Yes, we will be all right on this adventure."

But honestly, I was really scared too…

Fortunately the beautiful and powerful northern lights appeared in the sky to illuminate the dark at nightfall. We felt we were very small in a big forest.

We took our steps forward, toward the great unknown under the dancing northern lights.

We walked forward and joked with each other, laughing about how great heroes we were.

After wandering for a few days we did not know anymore where we had come from or where we were heading to. Eventually we arrivied at the edge of a cliff. A green pond was reflected below.

I stared at the pond. I heard in my ears, how the big salmon called to me to come. My brother warned me, saying that our mother warned us about this pond. I did not listen. The pond assured me that it would offer the world's best and biggest salmon.

I was sure that I would get down safely. Soon both of us would get lots of tasty salmon to eat.

However, after few steps, the boulder came loose beneath of my paws. I rolled down the hill, together with the boulder.

At first I felt the pain. Soon, everything went black.

I had hit my head badly. My paws hurt as I opened my eyes. The smell of the poison and contaminated salmon got to my nostrils. I was sure that I would not survive. My paws were so sore that I could not walk. Tears flowed down my cheeks. I should have listened to my mother´s and my brother's warning. I was scared.

Fortunately, my brother came up with an idea to help me. At nightfall, my brother called to the northern lights for their assistance. My brother made a lasso out of them, which he threw around me. After getting the lasso tight, my brother brought me back to the top of the cliff.

I was alive and far away from the toxic pond.

However, I could not walk for several days. Would we never get home? We were really homesick. When we were hungry in an unknown forest, our father prayed every day that we would survive. Our mother and our sister went out to look for us every day.

We were starving. We thought that our end would come before my paw would heal.

We heard a shrill sound from above and were alarmed. A big bird was flying near us. I wondered: will it strike? Fear crept into us again.

But, instead, it was an unknown osprey, who brought us salmon to eat.

The osprey told us that it knew where our Home Forest was. That it had seen from above one big bear talking about its two lost cubs, with paws crossed and tears in its` eyes. The osprey showed us the right direction with its wing, where we would find the Home Forest.

We were grateful for this unexpected assistance that we experienced. My paw healed. We continued our journey towards the Home Forest.

Alert but tired we wandered back home with my brother. However, inside of us bubbled the hope and joy of getting home.

After several paw steps we began to feel ashamed of our adventure.

Mother cried aloud as we approach the Home Forest. Mother did not recognize us from afar, because the scents of distant forests and waters had stuck on us.

However, soon she recognized us and greeted us with joy.

Our father was mad at us because we had gone our own way. But deep down he was happy that we had come back alive.

We asked for forgiveness from him that we did not obey. Now we understood why we had been warned. Something really bad could have happened to us.

We rejoiced together: we were home again! We held a party and played together.

Now that we were at home, we had food to eat. We had beloved ones around us.

We felt safe and loved. We grew, and got wisdom.

There is a lot to see out in the world, but the most important things you can usually find near by.

It is important to be loved.

Our story will be told among the bears —
always as the northern lights appear.